EMMA
Every Day

Roller Skating Worries

by C.L. Reid

illustrated by Elena Aiello

PICTURE WINDOW BOOKS

a capstone imprint

Published by Picture Window Books, an imprint of Capstone
1710 Roe Crest Drive, North Mankato, Minnesota 56003
capstonepub.com

Library of Congress Cataloging-in-Publication Data
Names: Reid, C. L., author. | Aiello, Elena (Illustrator), illustrator. |
Reid, C. L. Emma every day.
Title: Roller skating worries / by C. L. Reid ; illustrated by Elena Aiello.
Description: North Mankato, Minnesota : Picture Window Books,
an imprint of Capstone, [2021] | Series: Emma every day |
Audience: Ages 5-7. | Audience: Grades K-1. |
Summary: Emma's best friend Izzie loves roller skating,
and she is going to teach Emma; Emma is worried about falling
and hurting herself and her nerves make her wobbly—but Izzie
is sure that listening to their favorite music will help her relax
and forget her nerves. Includes an ASL fingerspelling chart,
glossary, and content-related questions.
Identifiers: LCCN 2021006129 (print) | LCCN 2021006130 (ebook) |
ISBN 9781663909220 (hardcover) | ISBN 9781663921895 (paperback)
| ISBN 9781663909190 (pdf) Subjects: LCSH: Deaf children—Juvenile
fiction. | Cochlear implants—Juvenile fiction. | Roller skating—Juvenile
fiction. | Best friends—Juvenile fiction. | CYAC: Deaf—Fiction. | Cochlear
implants—Fiction. | People with disabilities—Fiction. | Roller skating—
Fiction. | Best friends—Fiction. | Friendship—Fiction. Classification: LCC
PZ7.1.R4544 Ro 2021 (print) | LCC PZ7.1.R4544 (ebook) | DDC [E]—dc23
LC record available at https://lccn.loc.gov/2021006129
LC ebook record available at https://lccn.loc.gov/2021006130

Image Credits: Capstone: Daniel Griffo, 28, 29 top left, Margeaux
Lucas, 29 bottom right, Mick Reid, 29 top right, 29 bottom left

Design Elements: Shutterstock: achii, Mari C, Mika Besfamilnaya

Special thanks to Evelyn Keolian for her consulting work.

Designer: Tracy Davies

Printed in the United States   4890

TABLE OF CONTENTS

MEET EMMA

EMMA CARTER
Age: 8 Grade: 3

SIBLING
one brother, Jaden
(12 years old)

PARENTS
David and Lucy

BEST FRIEND
Izzie Jackson

PET
a goldfish named Ruby

favorite color: **teal**
favorite food: **tacos**
favorite school subject: **writing**
favorite sport: **swimming**
hobbies: **reading, writing, biking, swimming**

FINGERSPELLING GUIDE

MANUAL ALPHABET

Aa   Bb   Cc   Dd   Ee

Ff   Gg   Hh   Ii   Jj

MANUAL NUMBERS

0   1   2   3

Emma is Deaf. She uses American Sign Language (ASL) to communicate with her family. She also uses a cochlear implant (CI) to help her hear some sounds.

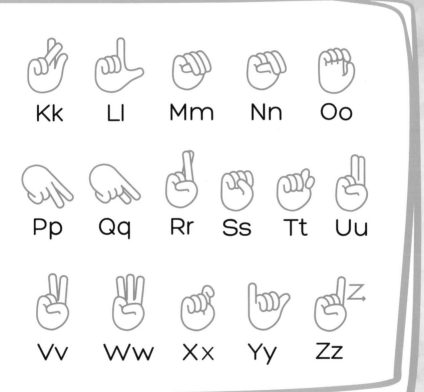

Kk Ll Mm Nn Oo

Pp Qq Rr Ss Tt Uu

Vv Ww Xx Yy Zz

4 5 6 7 8 9 10

Chapter 1
Gearing Up

Knee pads? Check. Elbow pads?

Check. Helmet? Check. New skates?

Check. Emma had all her gear.

She put on her cochlear implant

(CI) and talked to her pet fish, Ruby.

"I am scared. I don't want to

fall and hurt myself," she said.

Ruby  stopped

swimming and looked at Emma.

"You are right," Emma said.

"All I can do is try my best."

Emma grabbed her gear and went downstairs.

"You look ready to go!" Mom said, smiling.

"I'm nervous but excited," Emma signed.

"Have fun, and be careful," Mom signed.

"I will. Bye," Emma signed and skipped out the door.

It was a perfect spring day. Izzie was waiting outside. She already had all her gear on.

"Wow!  You look ready to skate," Emma signed.

"Yes! Now gear up so we can start

skating," Izzie signed.

Emma carefully put on all her

gear. Her helmet fit right over her CI.

Chapter 2
Shaky Skating

Izzie's driveway was wide and

flat. It was a great place to skate.

"I have never roller skated,"

Emma signed. "I am scared."

"That's okay. Just watch me,"

Izzie signed.

She stood up and skated off.

She gracefully glided down the

driveway. It looked easy.

Emma stood up. She teetered and

tottered and teetered and tottered.

Then she lost her balance and fell.

"Ouch!"  she cried.

Izzie skated back. "Are you

okay?" she signed.

"I am not hurt. My gear saved me," Emma signed.

Emma sat for a minute, taking a deep breath.

"I want to try again," she signed.

Emma stood and slowly started skating. But her legs felt very wobbly. She lost her balance and fell again.

"Ugh!" she cried.

"That was better!" Izzie said.

"It is hard, and I am still really

nervous," Emma signed.

"I have an idea," Izzie said.

Izzie helped Emma up and held
her elbow. They started to move
forward together.

But Emma was very shaky. After
only a few steps, Emma fell over.

"Ow!" 🤛✌️ Emma cried. She

blinked back tears.

Izzie plopped down next to her.

"I want to roller skate. I know I

can do it!" Emma signed.

Chapter 3

Beats and Balance

"I have another idea," Izzie

signed.

She took her skates off, ran into

her house, and came back with a

small speaker.

"Let's play our favorite music. Maybe that will help you relax," Izzie signed.

The music started. Emma's CI helped her hear it. Izzie danced in her skates. Emma laughed.

Emma stood up. She focused on the music. She forgot all about her wobbly legs and nerves.

Emma put her right foot in front
of her left. Then she put her left
foot in front of her right. She was
skating!

She felt steadier and stronger.

Izzie skated up to her. They skated

side-by-side around the driveway

a few times.

At the end of the song, they took

a break.

"Hooray!  You

did it!" Izzie said.

"Playing music was a great idea," Emma signed.

"Soon you will be dancing in your skates too," Izzie signed.

"Break time is over!" Emma signed. "Time to roll!"

LEARN TO SIGN

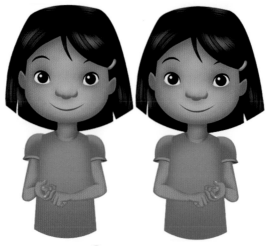

friend

1. Lock fingers.
2. Repeat with other hand on top.

congratulations

Clasp hands together and
shake twice.

scared

1. Make fists.
2. Open hands with palms facing chest.

dance

Move fingers back and forth over palm

roller skate

Bend two fingers and move hands back and forth.

music

Move hand back and forth along arm.

GLOSSARY

cochlear implant (also called CI)—a device that helps someone who is Deaf to hear; it is worn on the head just above the ear

deaf—being unable to hear

glide—to move smoothly and easily

fingerspell—to make letters with your hands to spell out words; often used for names of people and places

sign language—a language in which hand gestures, along with facial expressions and body movements, are used to communicate

steady—controlled

teeter—to sway back and forth

totter—to move in a shaky way

TALK ABOUT IT

1. Trying new things can be scary. How could you tell Emma was scared to try skating?

2. What are some of the things Izzie did to help Emma learn to skate? What else could she have tried?

3. Skating was hard for Emma, but she didn't give up. What did Emma do and say/sign to show that she wanted to keep trying?

WRITE ABOUT IT

1. Emma was scared to skate, but she didn't give up. Write down two things Emma said in the story to show her determination.

2. Make a list of at least five things you would like to try.

3. Izzie was a good skating teacher. Write down some words that describe what makes a good teacher.

Ruby

ABOUT THE AUTHOR

Deaf-blind since childhood, C.L. Reid received a cochlear implant (CI) as an adult to help her hear, and she uses American Sign Language (ASL) to communicate. She and her husband have three sons. Their middle son is also deaf-blind. C.L. earned a master's degree in writing for children and young adults at Hamline University in St. Paul, Minnesota. She lives in Minnesota with her husband, two of their sons, and their cats.

ABOUT THE ILLUSTRATOR

Elena Aiello is an illustrator and character designer. After graduating as a marketing specialist, she decided to study art direction and CGI. Doing so, she discovered a passion for illustration and conceptual art. She works as a freelancer for various magazines and publishers. Elena loves video games and sushi. She lives with her husband and her little pug, Gordon, in Milan, Italy.